DISNEY · PIXAR

# TOY STORY 4

# You've Got a Friend in Me

W9-BGA-624

By **Lauren Clauss**
Illustrated by **Jerrod Maruyama**

Random House New York

rhcbooks.com
ISBN 978-0-7364-4130-8
MANUFACTURED IN CHINA
10 9 8 7 6 5 4 3 2 1

Forky is a new toy. When Bonnie created him from trash, he didn't know about *anything*. Luckily, he has his fellow toys to help him. They teach him a lot about life, especially about **friendship**.

Forky learns how friendship comes in all shapes and sizes—

**big** and **small**,

**stuffed** and **plastic**!

Friends share their **hopes**

and **dreams** . . .

. . . and encourage each other

to follow their **hearts**!

With friends behind you as you

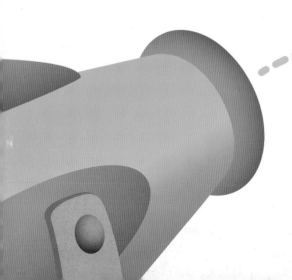

**aim**

for your goals, there's
no doubt you'll reach the

**stars**.

Friends will always be there to **hold you UP** . . .

. . . and they'll be right there
when you fall down.

Even if you have a bad day,

**friends** won't leave you.

Friends **never**

let friends go on adventures
# alone...

. . . even when those adventures get a little **scary**—

or **messy**!

By lending someone a hand,

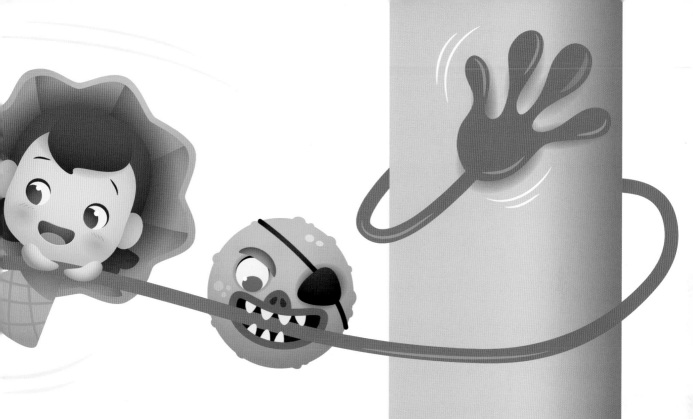

you may even make a
# new
# friend!

True friends are there for the

fun times . . .

. . . and they stick around for the bad times, too.

Friends always **believe** in you,

even when you want to **give up**.

Good friends **rush** to help, always encouraging you to

hang in there

Sometimes friends lose touch . . .
but they **never**

**forget**

each other.

Friends help you
**remember**

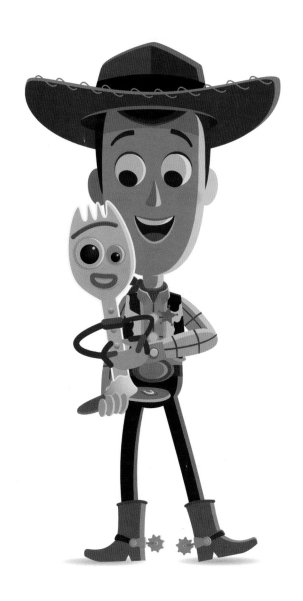

that everything will be **okay** in the end.

# Friendship is AMAZING!

And Forky knows he will always have great friends in Woody and the other toys.